CW00552861

RAMMblings

An anthology of musings from Devon writers

by

Chudleigh Writers' Circle

Chudleigh Phoenix Publications

A Chudleigh Phoenix Publications book

Copyright © Chudleigh Writers' Circle 2013

Edited by Sharon Cook and Margaret Mason
Illustration by Sharon Cook
Typeset by Kate McCormick

All rights reserved

No part of this publication may be reproduced, stored in a
retrieval system, or transmitted, in any form or by any means,
without the prior permission in writing of the publisher, nor be
otherwise circulated in any form of binding or cover other than
that in which it is published and without a similar condition
including this condition being imposed on the subsequent
purchaser.

ISBN: 978-0-9569508-3-3

Printed by Hedgerow Print, Crediton, Devon EX17 1ES

Contents

Acknowledgements

We owe very many thanks to: Maryon Avery, who organised the day out which sparked this anthology; Rob Mackenzie of RAMM, who listened to us; Chris and Alex for proofing and supporting.

Forword

It is always a delight to see how RAMM serves as an inspiration to others: writers and artists seem particularly drawn to our new displays. Museums in their purest form serve as a zone of engagement between objects and people. It's an experience that should stimulate new thoughts and ideas, start conversations and encourage debates. For some, such as the members of Chudleigh Writers' Group, it provided a spark of imagination that led to this anthology. I hope that this collection, along with the contents of RAMM's galleries, continues to inspire similar acts of creativity.

Julien Parsons
Senior Collections Officer, RAMM

Introduction

When a bunch of Chudleigh writers met up on a bright sunny morning in the autumn of 2012, none of us could have known just how inspiring the day was to become.

Our aim was to visit RAMM to wander, gaze and take pleasure in the vast array of artefacts, then write about a particular object which captured our imagination.

Later that day, over sausage sandwiches and lunch boxes — reminiscent themselves of summer days and adventures — we wrote and shared our offerings.

Ball gowns waltzed their way back in time, a piece of silver sparked a family history discussion, three gold bracelets told of love, a humble sampler spoke of tragedy, a seal skin parka harked back to hunting tales laced with sadness. Even an Anderson shelter provoked childhood memories.

A piece of lace, an Italian harpsichord, a Maori cloak, an Asian door hanging, and a ceiling all gave us tales of times past and lives lived.

But most of all our writers remembered the animals, in poetry and prose, their past selves speaking as their families created personal histories within the very confines of RAMM itself.

Two in particular jumped out. Both remember Gerald the Giraffe — one with fondness the other with the sadness of a free spirit who wants such a majestic creature to once again walk tall and free.

We offer you our RAMMblings, and seek little but your own pleasure in the past.

Dare you enter the museum of a million thoughts? ...

Des Shears, whose historical knowledge of Chudleigh and its environs makes him a much revered member of the group (he makes us laugh a lot), spoke of a vastly different building to the one he had taken his own daughters, Debbie and Teresa, to visit some forty years ago.

'I remember the girls were awestruck,' wrote Des, *'...Debbie read the inscription at the base of an exhibit and remarked "Gosh dad, it's even older than you," then sheepishly added, "but you've weathered better".*

'Switching my mind again to the present I made my way slowly up through this impressive building, marvelling at the collection of artefacts on view. Then I found myself amongst the collection of stuffed mammals. My mind did another trip down memory lane. Would the mammal Teresa had so much admired as a child still be there after so many years, namely the giraffe?

'Yes, it was still there on display, with that haughty look as it gazed down on its more inferior cousins. Teresa was of an age when anything is possible, which prompted this request. "Daddy, if you bought it it could live in our spare room."

'Standing amongst all those larger-than-life animals I tried to explain to the girls that giraffes do not fit comfortably into a bungalow.

'Flippantly Debbie added to the discussion by suggesting if a few roof tiles were removed it could look out and check when the school bus was coming.

'These last few remarks successfully brought the discussion to a close. We had almost forgotten the giraffe had been dead for years.'

Manny Lewis also remembered the same exhibit, but her fondness was tinged with a present day sadness.

'Gerald, as I remember him, standing tall commanding the space welcoming young and old into the entrance of the museum,' wrote Manny.
'Gerald was an old favourite and above all I wanted to reconnect with him. Gerald was, in 1989, the cornerstone of my

*experience when I first visited the museum at the start of my
working in Devon.*

　　*'Everything changed on this visit. I marvelled at the
transformation of the museum — the colour, the space, the
attention to detail. But where was Gerald? The main object of
my visit was nowhere to be seen. I searched everywhere, in all
the rooms and chambers.'*

　　When she found Gerald, Manny was disappointed: *'To
my sadness, in no way was he walking tall. He was trapped
within a darkened area. An area that seemed hostile. On one
side stood an Italian harpsichord, on the other an African bull
elephant captured from it natural environment. Gerald was
without dignity. There was no natural light. The habitat was
sterile, no long grasses, no trees, no companions of any kind.
Kilimanjaro was just a distant memory. No magical colours
touching the sky and beyond. Gerald had lost his magnitude and
power. He had lost his height. His voice was but a whisper. I left
the attic without looking back.'*

So powerful is Gerald he had, once again, assumed the power of
life to yet another visitor. Manny, along with Des's daughter,
wanted to take Gerald home, give him space to stand tall and
walk free.

How magical a museum can instil such power into its exhibits!
How grand it can still stir emotion, imagination and strength of
feeling within its revamped confines.

　　We hope you enjoy our RAMMblings. And hope they
might — just might — inspire your own visit. What will you
find?

Sharon Cook, Chair of Chudleigh Writers Circle
with excerpts from Des Shears and Manny Lewis

That Day Out At RAMM
Roger Brandon

Our spirits were high and the weather was fine,
We were all looking forward to such a good time.
'Now don't miss the bus, that would be such a pity.'
On our day out at RAMM in Exeter City.

They have hundreds of creatures, some big and some small.
With elephants wide and Gerald so tall,
And everyone liked the big Bengal kitty.
On that day out at RAMM in Exeter City.

We all chose an object and sat down to write;
It could be quite serious or it might be quite light,
And one wrote some verse which was really quite witty.
On that day out at RAMM in Exeter City.

Imagine that you are an Inuit hunter,
Or a centurion from Hadrian's junta.
Standing engrossed, just like Walter Mitty,
On that day out at RAMM in Exeter City.

You might write a bit about Exeter jail,
Or the washed up bones of a Cuvier's whale,
Or some Honiton lace that is marvellously pretty.
On that day out at RAMM in Exeter City.

Or how about a Roman tiled floor,
Or the fossilised bones of a Ichthyosaur,
That looks like it was designed by committee.
On that day out at RAMM in Exeter City.

Some went for fiction and made up a tale,
And some stuck to fact as straight as a nail,
Some mixed them both in a story quite gritty,
On that day out at RAMM in Exeter City.

Some wrote in prose and some wrote in verse,
They were really quite good but mine was much worse,
I just sat and penned this poor little ditty.
On that great day at RAMM in Exeter City.

Three Gold Bracelets

Jean Grimsey

The round hut with its turfed roof was dark and smelled of smoke. The only light, from the narrow entrance, hardly reached the back of the single room where, head bent in anticipated sorrow, a tired work-worn man stood watching a dying woman. Her left hand worried at the gold bracelet wrapped around her thin, bony right wrist, pulling at it, tugging, fretting. He bent nearer to catch the murmured words from her dry lips.

'Do not...'

'Do not what, my love?'

'Do not bury it with me.'

She caught her breath, coughed, then struggled to speak again.

'Give it to the boy. Tell him to go and find a bride. It is for her, for the living.'

She sighed, a final soft exhalation. The man wept for the woman lost and for the boy child, not yet ten, who stood in the shadows, watching.

Now the child was motherless, like so many other children in their tribe. He had no thoughts of taking a bride, of wooing her with his mother's bracelet. His mother was the only woman he had loved, and she was gone. The boy struggled to understand the finality of death.

The man pulled gently at the bracelet. Soft gold, malleable, it bent to his strength, just as it had all those years ago when he had fashioned it for her from a simple rod of gold. He had given it to his woman at their first coming together, a token of love and promise. Now all her life was there, sat in the palm of his hand, a coil of precious metal, shell-like, its value far more than mere gold and workmanship.

They buried the woman at dawn the following day, placing her with care in a round barrow near a small stone circle on the edge of the heath. She would not be alone; there were other barrows nearby holding the remains of her mother and her father. The man laid her down gently, her head to the south, her face facing to the west.

'Now you can still see the setting sun,' he whispered as he placed around her the things she had used in life: a pottery bowl and a jar of oil, the cup she drank from and the comb he had fashioned for her. Some of the elders spoke of an afterlife where the dead would need such things so the tribe did what they could for their dead.

Life went on and the man took another wife and fathered more children. He hid the gold bracelet in a pottery jar, keeping it safe for his eldest son as his first love had wished. There were no gold bracelets for his second woman, she was there to cook and weave and give birth to children, not to love.

In time his work as a metal smith made him an important man as he traded the goods he worked in copper, gold and bronze for jars of oil and animal pelts, adding to the wealth and comfort of his family and the other members of the tribe.

Now his son had grown to be a man working alongside his father, and it was time to do what his mother had wished and find himself a bride. The woman he chose was the eldest daughter of the local chief, a man of great power and wealth, almost a king. To woo and win such a woman would take more than one simple gold bracelet, however finely wrought. Together the father and son began work on two further bracelets fashioning simple bands of gold, their ends folded back so that, torque-like, they could be slipped upon a slender wrist and bent to shape and fit. Heating the gold, then hammering it to a perfect smoothness would take time, time they had to snatch from their everyday work so progress was slow. Whilst the son pursued his love the father worked on the bracelets, storing them for safety in the same jar that held that first gold band.

The tribal chief was unprepared for what happened next. Complaisant in his life, comfortable with his

wealth and position as the leader of the peaceful farming
community, he ignored the rumours about other warring tribes.
These came from the west where the land could no longer
support the growing numbers so starving men headed east,
plundering the land and killing those who stood in their way.
The metalsmith, perhaps wiser, saw the threat and took the jar
with its precious bracelets and buried it in a hole in the ground,
up near the barrow where his first wife lay. Maybe he hoped that
a deep-seated fear of death would keep the jar safe from the
marauders.

He showed his eldest son where he had buried the
hoard.

'Take note of where the jar is hidden. Your
mother willed that one bracelet to your bride, the others we will
finish when we can.'

'I will remember, father. The jar is there, near my
mother, she will watch over it. And when the danger is passed
we can start work again.'

But the danger never went away. The incoming
warring tribes massacred the chief and all his family, leaving the
smith's son to mourn his bride-to-be. The bracelet from his dead
mother was never slipped onto the wrist of his living bride, his
mother's wish was unfulfilled.

Disaster followed disaster as the tribe, weakened by
fighting, starvation and the cold, succumbed to fever. It took the
man and his son, his woman and all his other children too,
leaving no-one to disinter the hidden jar.

So the bracelets lay in the cold, dark soil until time unearthed
them, and they saw the light of day. They glinted in the same
sun that warmed the earth thousands of years ago, three rings of
gold, each one fitting within the next, a shell-like coil of
precious metal. Now they are displayed, treasure trove for us to
view and covet, and perhaps make up stories as to who and
when and why.

Did You Know?

Susan Thompson

Oh Best Beloveds
Did you know
That in South Devon long ago
The reptiles Rynchosaurs roamed
Eating plants and quite at home?

In those days Britain now so called
Was nearer the Equator
So different from today
Two hundred and thirty five million years later!

Oh Best Beloveds
Did you know
That a mere hundred thousand years ago
Hippos and Elephants of yore
Dwelt in South Devon across the Moor
Which now we know can get very cold!
Would you believe it?
Well. It is just so.

Did you know
Best Beloveds
Are you also aware
That to keep them warm
The Polar Bears
Have black skin
Beneath their fur?
One lived to 95
Most rare!

And one more thing
Before I go
My Best Beloveds
For it is so
As a strictly proven matter of fact
That Giraffes have seven bones
In their neck at the back
Just like me and you
The only difference being
They have the Bird's Eye View!

Anna Smale's Sampler
Maryon Avery

My name is Anna Smale. I am eleven and a half and I live in
Exeter with my Ma, four brothers and one sister. I have another
brother, George. He's in the army and is over the sea in Canada.
My eldest sister, Ellen, is married and lives round the corner. Pa
died when I was seven.

I have just made a sampler. It's quite plain because after
I'd stitched the list of names and dates, there wasn't any space
for decoration. My Sunday school teacher, Miss Brown, gave
me this piece of linen. Nice, isn't it? The weave is very even.
She gave me the thread too, said brown would show up well
against the cream-coloured material.

You look puzzled. Are you wondering why a poor child
like me has made a sampler? Isn't it just the rich folk with time
on their hands who make such things, hands which are strangers
to hard work and which hardly ever get dirty?

Well, at Sunday School a couple of months ago, Miss
Brown was telling my class about how Jesus grew up in an
ordinary family (I expect his hands got dirty with all that
carpentry) and then she asked us about our own families. It took
quite a long time because everyone in my class comes from a
big family. When it was my turn, I started off all right but I
began to cry when I told her about my Pa who died four years
ago. This set the others off about their aunts and uncles and
cousins who had died around that time too. Usually grown-ups
tell us to be quiet when we talk about the people who died and
not to be so soft but Miss Brown is kind and she just let us talk.

Two or three days after that Miss Brown came round to
our house with this material and said I should make a sampler so
that our family doesn't forget the ones who had died. She'd
brought some paper and a pencil as well. We sat at the kitchen

table and planned out on paper what would go on my sampler; my family, names, dates of birth, dates of death.

I told Miss Brown what I knew and Ma and Ellen remembered what they could: George is the oldest, then come William, Ellen and Thomas, two years between each of them. Henry is next, Mary, then me and the littlest is Sidney. He's two years younger than me and right cheeky with it.

As we were talking, Ma remembered the names of little ones who had died before I was born. She got up and lifted her special box off the top shelf. I knew it was special because she'd told me it was where she kept important things. But I had never seen her open it before. She went through some papers and in a matter-of-fact voice read out the dates which she'd had trouble remembering - babies Alice, John and Fanny, then Elizabeth and Ann less than four years old. I'm good at sums and worked out Ma must have been having babies all the time, sometimes two a year! There could hardly have been room to move in our little house.

'Didn't you feel sad when your babies died, Ma?' I asked.

Ma laughed a short laugh. It wasn't an amused sort of laugh. She told me there wasn't any time to be sad. Too much to do looking after the living. Babies came. Sometimes they lived, sometimes they didn't. It was the way things were. Then Pa got sick and died and that was that.

I felt bold enough with Miss Brown there to ask Ma about the illness which had killed Pa. I'd tried asking before, but Ma usually gave me chores to do to shut me up.

'Cholera,' said Ma. 'We didn't know it at the time, but that was what it was right enough. He kept being sick and ...,' she fidgeted and looked embarrassed. '...And the other business. He couldn't eat or drink and just got worse and worse until there was nothing left of him and he died.'

'Was there nothing that could be done?' Miss Brown's voice was very gentle.

'That nice Dr Shapter came to see him when he was in this part of town,' said Ma. 'You must remember him. Came to Exeter in '32. 'Bout the only medical man we ever clapped eyes on. He did his best but Tom was just too sick. My God, hundreds of people died here that year. Dr Shapter said it wasn't our fault. He reckoned the disease was part and parcel of not having clean water.'

'I remember when we had to fetch water from the conduit in South Street,' Ellen chipped in. 'We used jugs, buckets, anything really to bring it to the house. It was river water. We had to wash ourselves and our clothes in it. It was already filthy dirty even before we started.'

Not to be left out I piped up, 'And I remember when I was little there was a really horrible smelly stream running down the middle of the road outside our house. You were always telling me to keep out of it, Ellen.'

'Where does your water come from now?' Miss Brown asked.

'The pump on the corner,' Ma told her with a proud smile. 'Comes in from the reservoir on the edge of the city. Beautiful it is. So clean it sparkles.'

I started my sampler that afternoon and worked on it whenever I had a minute. I finished it today. I hope it doesn't get lost.

∞∞∞∞∞∞∞∞∞∞

Cholera broke out in Exeter in 1832. Over 400 people died as a result. Dr Thomas Shapter wrote about it and contributed to the discovery that the disease spreads through polluted water. To prevent another outbreak, the authorities had a reservoir built to supply clean water to the city.

Anna Smale's sampler was completed on 8th June 1837. William IV died on 20th June 1837 and Victoria succeeded him.

A Twist in the Tale of John Elston 1670 — 1732
Anne Chinneck

Some of you may be familiar with the work of John Elston,
goldsmith and silversmith, some of whose exquisite work is on
display at the museum. My story is not a work of fiction but
more a story of a family reaching back 300 years.

This story is based on research into the Elston family
using a genealogy site and census records. As these go back
only as far as 1841, the years before this are quite difficult to
identify. The name of Elston is widespread across Devon, so I
had to rely on other old records to narrow down John Elston's
descendants.

It appears many of John Elston's family and forbears
lived in Morchard Bishop near Crediton. John Elston himself
worked in Exeter and became a Freeman of the city during his
lifetime. It is not clear where he worked but there is a record of
his being apprenticed to a John Verdon in 1691. John himself
later had several apprentices, one of whom was his son, Philip
Elston who was apprenticed in 1701. Philip died in 1755.

To go back earlier, John Elston's father was William
Elston, who died in 1675 and was married to Elizabeth, who
died in 1694, 19 years after her husband. Their burials are
registered in the area of Exeter West.

Amongst William Elston's children was another
William, married to Mary. They died in 1704 and 1714
respectively, also in Exeter. Their son was John Elston, who
went on to have such an illustrious career. I could only find a
record of his work amongst the church plate in Torrington
church, 1719. As you will see later, our family has a silver
spoon made by John. This is what started my research —
curiosity! Little did I know how difficult the task would be.

There is a gap in my research of a generation after Philip
died in 1755, although there is a record of another John Elston, a

sergemaker, who also became a Freeman of Exeter in 1741. The link is picked up again with William Elston who was born in 1803, married to Elizabeth, born in 1807. William died in 1865. After this date the ancestry becomes easier to trace with the use of census records.

One of William and Elizabeth's five children was Harriet Elston who was born in 1850 and lived until 1929. She married a John Carter Chinneck in St Luke's church in Torquay in 1873. John was an Inspector of Schools who died in 1887 in Newton Abbot. John's family came from the island of Jersey, where there is a clear record of this. John's father was also John. He married Ann Carter in 1844 in Jersey, The record of their marriage shows John Chinneck originally came from Portsmouth.

After their marriage John and Harriet went on to have seven children who all survived into adulthood. Family records show two of the children emigrated whilst four stayed in Dawlish, Devon. I have seen churchyard records there. John and Harriet's fourth child was Robert Percy, born in 1881. Robert married a Lydia Frost and they had two children, John Elston, born in 1907 and Muriel Winifred, born two years later. Unfortunately, Robert Percy died young in 1928, in East Grinstead.

Now the link between the Elston family and the Chinneck family becomes clear. John Elston Chinneck had five children, one of whom is Andrew who was born in 1942 at High Bullen near South Molten at the height of the 2nd World War. In 1966 Andrew married me, Anne Dickinson. We have three children: Jennifer Anne (1970); James Andrew Elston (1973); and Victoria Mary (1977).

And so the wheel turned full circle. The silver spoon made by John Elston in the 1700s must have come down from Harriet and is still in our possession. This is what started me on my research for this anthology, having seen and admired John Elston's silver in Exeter museum. We now know there have been Chinnecks in Devon for 400 years, from research conducted by another family member, Anthony Chinneck.

I don't pretend my research is 100% accurate and I know I have not given any references to validate my assumptions. It is just what I think happened. Someone out there may know different. If so, please let me know via The Chudleigh Writers' Circle.

A Wartime Experience: The Anderson Shelter
Marion Thomas

The noise that woke me was the distant whine of aircraft droning through the dark night sky. The sound grew louder as they approached, heading for the nearby ports of Southampton and Portsmouth. My mother suddenly burst into the bedroom and grabbed me from my bed. She thrust my arms into my dressing gown and my feet into cosy slippers.

'Quick,' she said, 'there'll be a raid shortly,' and practically dragged me down the stairs and out into the street. As we left the house the air-raid siren rang out its dire warning through the frosty air.

We headed for a neighbour's home a few doors away, clutching our gas masks. In the garden was an Anderson shelter around six feet high and built of corrugated iron, where we would remain until the "all clear" sounded. It was cunningly disguised beneath a grassy bank.

My father was an air-raid warden. He didn't join us in the shelter. Each evening he went off on patrol in his uniform cap and jacket. I used to wonder whether he was in danger and whether he would come back safely.

In the shelter several neighbours had already gathered, mostly women and elderly men, plus an assortment of children and babies. The shelter was furnished with a couple of not very comfortable wooden benches, lanterns, blankets, a supply of water and a potty. The women discussed the miserly rations we were allocated: a mere two ounces of tea, cheese and fat for the week, plus four ounces of bacon, twelve of sugar and four of margarine. They exchanged details of ways they had discovered of eking out these meagre supplies. I dozed on my mother's knee until the murmur of voices faded.

I was awoken by the "all clear" siren and we then dispersed to our homes for a welcome sleep, but these nightly trips were to become a feature of my early years. In the morning I would peer out of the window into the street, watching the endless convoys of lorries, tanks and military jeeps passing. Behind them marched a procession of hundreds of weary troops. I wondered where they were heading, what they would be doing and whether I should ever get to join them when I grew up.

We were told that Hitler was furious because British planes had bombed Lübeck and in retaliation he had ordered historic English towns to be targeted. Looking back down the years since those childhood days it seems hard to believe that these events took place during my lifetime. Yet even now the far-off sound of a military aeroplane has the power to remind me. After nearly sixty years of peace in our country we should not forget; these memories are important.

Of Mice and Elephants
Colin Avery

Grey,
the intermediate colour
between dark and light,
between black and white,
between day and night.

Grey,
the indeterminate colour
of school trousers,
of unwashed shirts.
of grime and grease,
of granite and gravel,
of mice and elephants.

Grey,
the indistinct colour
of winter skies,
of thunder clouds,
of porridge and maggots,
of pigeons and parrots (well, the grey ones, anyway).

Grey,
the sombre colour
of most of the walls,
the floors,
the ceilings,
the windows,
the pillars,
the blinds
and some of the visitors
in the Royal Albert Memorial Museum.

But

that neutral colour in between
the hidden bits and exhibits
turns attention from itself
to halls of history,
textile and gown,
to walls of Widgery,
Turner and Towne,
to galleries of arty effects,
to archaeological artefacts,
to educational figures and facts,
and the museum café for drinks and snacks
in the Royal Albert Memorial Museum.

The First Hunt
Elizabeth Ducie

It's still dark when he awakes and no-one else is stirring in the barabara. He can hear the sounds of slumber from the other families and wonders what it would be like to live in a small dwelling with just his mother. He thinks they would be lonely very soon.

There's been so much to do in the past few days preparing for the hunt. By the time the sun went down the previous day, they were all exhausted. His mother lit the oil in the soap-stone lamp and they ate their supper by its smoky light. He saw her glance at him several times, clutching at the enamel cross she always wears, but she said nothing and neither did he.

The parka was next to his bed when he went to his sleeping quarters. He'd never seen it before, but he knew its story. His mother had told him many times.

The ships appeared on the horizon one day late in the spring. We knew they were coming to hunt sea otter and the clan was divided. The elders were unhappy the strangers would be taking our animals and not giving us much in return. Old Anna talked of new diseases brought by these strangers. She was the Wise Woman who advised frightened young mothers before they gave birth for the first time. It was she who washed the old folk before they went to their final resting places far from the settlement. When Anna spoke, people listened.

But to the youngsters, it was an exciting time. The boys hoped to learn new skills and show off to the girls but we were not interested in watching them while such handsome strangers were around.

I was sitting outside the shelter helping your grandmother prepare a whale skin when the prickle on the back of my neck told me we were not alone. He was leaning against a

rock on the other side of the clearing, watching us. When I
looked up, he bowed his head slightly and I heard your
grandmother sigh. I put down my scraper, smiled at her and took
the path to the shore. I knew he would follow me.

His eyes were the colour of the sea in autumn when the
late afternoon sun shines on the water. He was tall, even taller
than your grandfather who was known in the clan as *Touch Sky*.
When we stood together, I barely reached his shoulder.

Ivan knew only a few words of *Unangan* to start with,
but we talked with our hands, with signs, with pictures in the
sand. He drew a map of his home in far-off Russia. He talked of
the treacherous journeys they made each year, sailing south east
to *Nawan-Alaxsxa*. This land of ours some call Aleutia but to
him it was the Catherine Islands, named after their great
empress. He also told me of his God who sent Christ, his son, to
save us all but I knew those stories already.

When I was little, I went to Father Herman's school and
learnt about the angels and saints. The old monk had given up
running the school by then and was living on Spruce Island.
Herman wanted to be a hermit, said he needed to be alone with
God, but every Sunday and on Feastdays, crowds of people
would sail across the little stretch of water to visit and pray with
him. Your grandparents took me once and I remember him as a
gentle, quiet man, bent over his stick, stopping to talk to all the
children as he walked to his chapel for mass.

I think Ivan would have been a priest if he'd had the
choice. He wasn't like the other men who came on the ships.
Every night, when they returned from hunting, they would sit
outside their tents laughing loudly, drinking the colourless spirit
they brought with them from home, and eating the food we gave
them. As the evenings wore on, the noise would rise, laughter
would turn to shouting and the wise among us would crawl into
our homes and hope to remain undisturbed. But each night,
some of the women would go to the tents to keep the visitors
company.

Ivan was one of their leaders. He told me he couldn't stop the men having their fun after a long day's hunt, but he made sure your grandmother and I were never bothered. Each evening he ate supper with us. After we retired, he would sit outside our door, reading in the firelight until the noise died down and the hunters fell asleep.

One day he told me he was leaving. The hunting season was over and they needed to sail home before the sea began to freeze, as it did each winter. That night we walked upon the beach. The moon was full, its light making a broad pathway across the water. Away from the settlement, we could hear no noise save the waves on the sand. He begged me to go home with him, but I was too frightened. I couldn't leave your grandparents alone. I couldn't go to a strange country where I feared most people would be like his hunters and not like him. I cried as I shook my head and in the moonlight, I could see tears on his cheeks too. Then for the last time, we lay together on the sand.

I didn't watch them sail away. I hid in the settlement until your grandmother returned from the shoreline, carrying the enamel cross I'd seen so often around his neck - and his promise to return the next year. I squeezed it tight within my fist and as the two cross bars bit into my palm, I hoped this pain would take away the other.

I began to make the parka that same day, my present to him on his return. It was to keep him warm and dry when hunting, so bird skin would not do. That year, there was a good catch of seals. Your grandfather would bring the carcasses home and the skins were soaked in urine to stretch them before your grandmother and I could start to sew. The meat kept us fed throughout the winter and I claimed the guts for the parka. I turned them inside out to scrape away the tissue and fat. Then I fastened them to stakes and left them to dry until they were ready to be sewn. My needle was made of bone and I used fish gut as thread. I decorated the sleeves and the hem with strips of cloth dyed vermillion and squid-ink black. Along the seams I stitched feathers, seal bristles and caribou hair for luck. I knew Ivan did not believe in the power of animal spirits, but I hoped his God would forgive me and understand. Finally, I stitched some of my own hair across the shoulders. That way, I could be with him even during the hunt.

The parka took many months to finish. The winter was over and the clan was starting to talk of spring and the return of the hunters by the time it was ready. It was so stiff it could stand on its own and, like him, it was taller than me..

But of course, my son, the parka was not the only thing I made that winter. Like many of the women in the clan, my belly swelled. Before the pain of my first tattoo had faded, there came a day when Old Anna and your grandmother sat with me and held my hands as you were born. I screamed and cried as you thrust your way into the world and prayed you would be a great hunter like your father.

The ships returned soon after I placed the parka outside the entrance to our dwelling so Ivan would see it as he entered the settlement. Then I wrapped you in a bird skin blanket and took you to the shore to meet your father.

I watched as all the men came off the ships. There were many Russian faces, some we recognised from the year before, others were new, but his was not there. I told myself he would be the last to appear, he must wait until the end, make sure everyone was safely off. Then I told myself he must have left early before I arrived; he would be waiting for me at the settlement. I hurried back home. But the settlement was empty, as I knew it would be.

That night I wrapped the parka in blankets and put it away. I married the man you call Papa the following year. He's been good to me and you, my Russian child. I have made many garments since, but no-one has ever worn your father's parka. It was made for a special hunter and only a special hunter will wear it.

He lies in the darkness and dreams of visiting a far-off land. There have been many visitors over the years and they have told tales of deep winters, wolves, churches with golden domes and towns with more people than he can imagine in one place at one time.

On the other side of the grass curtain, he hears his mother stir. Other voices talk quietly in the communal cooking area as the clan begins to wake.

Herman Ivanovych rises from his bed and prays that his first hunt will be successful. He hopes he will be worthy of his mother's faith in him and that his father, wherever he is, will be proud of him.

Nineteenth Century Hoodie
Elizabeth Ducie

It's mighty cold in the Aleutian Isles
We need to wrap up warm
A hand-made parka is just the thing
For hunting in a storm

It's made from the guts of a sea-mammal
With lining stitched in rows
It's thick, it's long, it stretches past my knees
But not quite to my toes

It takes a year for mother to make one
She really hates to sew
She trims it with red ribbon and her hair
Then says 'now please don't grow'

The Ball Gown: An Unfinished Romance
Margaret Barnes

'Will he notice me? He must,' Sophia said. Her breath coming in short bursts as her maid, Anna, pulled tight the corset round her waist.

The invitation to the Big House had arrived six weeks ago. A large stiff card edged in gold with her name written on it in a careful round hand.

'*Sir William and Lady Goldbrough would like the pleasure of your company at a Grand Ball on 23rd October 1883 at 9pm.*'

Sophia's immediate reaction had been one of ennui. Country balls were so, well, boring. Young girls twittering and giggling, awkward young men who trod on your toes and talked of hunting and fishing; so tedious after the excitement of a season in London. But that had been four years ago.

Her father had grumbled at the expense of her time in the city, and if her mother had not intervened he would have refused to pay for the dresses and gowns she needed. When she came home without receiving a single proposal of marriage, or at least not one she was prepared to admit to, he continued to make clear he begrudged the expenditure. One man had proposed to her. But no matter how many times she had told herself it might be the only chance she got, the man was so ugly she had refused him. She kept the offer secret, knowing her father would be furious she had declined.

Sophia had gracefully accepted the invitation to The Ball. It would make a change from the dances in the local hotel and she had put the card on her mantelpiece, where it leant on the mirror behind a small china pug. She would consider what to wear nearer the time. Then Anna told her she had met one of the maids from The Big House in the village,

'They're all at sixes and sevens at the Hall. He's so handsome, quite makes them all aflutter,' Anna said.

'Who's that?' Sophia asked.

'Mr Robert. He's back from Canada. And,' Anna paused, 'he's worth six thousand pounds a year.'

Robert — Sir William's youngest son — and Sophia had been childhood playmates, running around the estate, playing in the streams and ponds and climbing trees until he went, first to Eton then to Oxford. They saw each other when he came home on vacation, but had slowly drifted apart as he became more sophisticated. She had remained stuck here in this rural backwater. And now he was back.

'Is his wife with him?' she had asked.

'No, Miss Sophia. He's not married. Yet.' Anna had pulled the brush hard, straightening the tangles of Sophia's strawberry blonde hair, making her wince.

When Anna had left her, Sophia went to her wardrobe and searched through her ball dresses. She took out first one, then another, throwing them across her bed. She needed a new gown; something so beautiful everyone in the room would admire her.

She said nothing for a couple of days then, when she thought her father was in a good mood, she went down to breakfast early.

'You're early,' her father said, as she sat down at the table. She picked up her napkin and placed it on her knees.

'Yes, I wanted to ask you about something.'

He looked at her over his newspaper, but said nothing. Sophia took a slice of toast from the rack and began to butter it.

'It's the Goldbrough's Ball. Are you and Mama going?'

Her father ignored the question.

'I'm sure you're really looking forward to it. I know I am. If only I had a new gown,' Sophia sighed. 'I really do need a new ball gown.'

'What's wrong with those you had for London? Won't one of those do?' He turned his attention back to his paper again.

'Those old things. No. No. I need something more fashionable now I'm older.'

'You need a husband to pay your bills,' he said from behind his newspaper.

She let him continue reading and nibbled on her slice of toast.

'Robert's back from Canada.' She paused. 'Unmarried.'

Her father looked up at her then folded his newspaper and placed it by the side of his plate. Without looking up, he picked up a letter from the small pile of papers in front of him and slid the blade of his knife through the envelope to open it. He pulled out a sheet of notepaper, read the contents and began to work his way through the rest of the envelopes. Sophia sat quietly; he was not to be pushed. Pleading would do no good. She knew her father would only pay for a ball gown if he believed it was worthwhile.

The minutes dragged and then he said, 'Your mother will only nag at me if I don't agree. So go and see your dressmaker. But don't spend too much money.'

'Thank you, Papa.' She went over and stood behind his chair, put her arms round his neck, and kissed the top of his bald head.

The parlour of Mrs Haworth's house was stuffed with fabrics, silk, satins and velvet as well as the more homely cottons, worsteds and linens. Hanging out of the drawers were ribbons of every conceivable colour. Piled on a table were rolls of intricate lace and beads of all sizes and shapes. Sophia touched the silks, her hand lingering against the soft fabrics. She held up a piece to her face to gauge the effect on the colour of her skin and eyes.

'Blue. I think blue. What do you think, Mrs Haworth?' Sophia said to the little dumpling of a dressmaker.

Mrs Haworth held out a swatch of midnight blue.

'Something lighter, nearer the colour of my eyes,' said Sophia

The dressmaker searched through a pile of cloth before producing a fine corded silk, the colour of a summer sky.

Sophia sighed deeply. 'Yes, that's it.'

'And the bodice and underskirt of cream,' said Mrs Haworth. 'I have just the thing.'

She dived into a cupboard and pulled out a bolt of figured silk satin in two shades of cream.

'There, hold that against your skin.'

Sophia took it and held it against her cheek. Her face took on the bloom of a fresh pink rose. The silk was soft and tactile, irresistible - just what she was looking for.

'We'll cut the bodice just so,' said Mrs Haworth running her finger so it just crossed the top of Sophia's breasts. 'The overdress we'll cut like a coat, with points just here.' She pointed to hip-level.

'And a train?' enquired Sophia

'Yes, of course. Just like the London fashions.'

'Now for trimming the bodice, I've got these.' Mrs Haworth bobbed down and opened a bottom drawer. She pulled out a roll of net embellished with glass beads, the shape of maple leaves.'

Stood in front of the mirror in her bedroom, wearing the gown Sophia studied her appearance with great satisfaction.

'He will notice me,' she whispered to herself.

31

Almost a Dome
Maryon Avery

To attempt to square the circle is
An exercise in futility
which can almost be done.
Almost, but not quite.

The transition from square to circle is also
impossible.

Yet corbelling, vaulting,
complex geometry and
proportional relationship -
the regular geometry
that holds true throughout -
makes the square tessellation of half and quarter star octagons
look like a dome.

A corbelled pyramid
is almost a dome.
Almost, but not quite.

Futility or beauty?

Poetic language was used to describe Muqarnas, the term given
to an architectural device unique to Islamic architecture.

Sodi's Harpsichord 1782
Margaret Mason

'It is exquisite,' said Thomas, as he ran his slim ageing fingers along the soft blue background. 'Quite exquisite.'

Shafts of morning sunlight pierced the little windows of a London music shop, their sparkling brightness dancing across Thomas' wrinkled cheek and grey hair. He stretched his aching shoulder bones to touch the radiant blue sheen.

'Indeed it is, Sir. You will note the delicate artistry of the painter in these countryside scenes. See, here, most especially upon the lid.' The diminutive shopkeeper encouraged him to step closer to the harpsichord. His extravagant arm gestures explaining the value of the piece, 'Here, on this edge and in this beautiful curve, do you see how the ships glide upon the waters?'

He pointed to the galleon's majestic sails, their dip and bob upon a swelling sea luring Thomas to believe and sway with their motion. Thomas touched the sails, felt the freedom of the breezes that beckoned the travellers and nodded his agreement.

'Yes, yes I do see your meaning, Sir. And tell me of its tone,' said Thomas. He moved to the keys, placed a finger upon the first, studying its carved perfection, noting each one as a mirror image of the next. With a quick nudge against Thomas' arm the little shopkeeper slipped on to the leather stool, before Thomas had a chance to flick his coat tails and sit there himself.

Quick, echoing tones came sighing from the strings. A light intoxicating melody stole Thomas' imagination and led him to float upon its pure sound. Thomas removed his hand, continued along the case and stepped beside the raised lid, drawn there by the fine paintings. He paused to search the scene. The shopkeeper played on, the notes rising and falling in sweet accompaniment to the tall ships.

The soft eyes of a country woman stared from the lid and seemed to beckon to Thomas to join her. He felt certain he saw her smile and raise a hand to encourage him to sit. As he looked he felt he knew this place, its tall trees, its grassy banks. The woman too, seemed familiar. She bore the look of his mother with her dark hair, pale complexion and ready smile.

'And what do you think of it, Sir?' said the shopkeeper continuing to play. 'How does it feel, can you hear its call?'

The question broke Thomas' concentration. Lines of taut strings inside the harpsichord's case interrupted him with their increasing vibration. He looked inside and studied the movements, rising in tempo now, the echoing within the case proving everything the shopkeeper had said. He moved around the farther end of the harpsichord, noting its five bulbous legs, their decorations heavy with sky blue, broken only by swirling fulsome roses intertwined within their golden frames.

Thomas approached him, 'In all my years I have never seen such an instrument, Sir. It surpasses my expectations in every way — in decoration, in tone, in emotion.'

The closer he looked, the more the music rose and the more he felt at one with the sounds and the scenes.

As he stared he saw the woman's hand rise as if in farewell to someone on the ship, now rigged to full sail. 'That white horse', he murmured, 'is it not Titan, his white mane and tail flicking in so distinctive a manner?' His father had given this horse to his elder brother, Benjamin. Here was Benjamin in the saddle, riding, waving and holding back the reins, his shoulders arched in sorrow beneath his red cloak, and he, still land bound upon his white horse.

Thomas watched drawn in by the scene and borne up by the music. Deeper memories raced in, flooding him and filling his eyes with tears. There, there on the ship, his fingers rose to touch the man standing, straining to see, to look back, a man in distress. Thomas's fingers reached out, 'Father,' he murmured, 'Father,' he said again as he touched the figure.

'And what do you feel now, Sir?' said the shopkeeper, still busy at the keys. 'Is it not the most incredible piece?'

Thomas' attention never wavered from his father, and as if from another place he heard his voice answer, 'I have never felt such an instrument, Sir. It is a most captivating piece.'

The shopkeeper's deft fingering and mesmeric melody absorbed Thomas. He found himself returning to stand beside the open case, drawn back to the strings; his eyes fixed upon their motion their lilting echoes lifting him away. He noted a glance from the shopkeeper, an intriguing expression, a smile inching across his face as he continued to play, his fingers now appearing to be at one with the pale wooden keys moving as their extension.

Thomas' gaze returned to the ship, to the shore, to the single horse. With damp eyes he reached to touch the white horse. He felt Titan's flank, his warm rippling muscles. He stretched again, more easily now, and entwined his fingers in his brother's red cloak, 'Ben, Ben,' he whispered.

The horsemen turned, his face full of sadness, his deep eyes cloudy. A gloved hand reached down and Thomas gripped his brother's fingers. His heart raced, a searing breath breathed in time with the rippling strings bore him up as hand and glove held fast. He felt Titan's muscles brace to haul him in. He blinked as the dark form of a second horse emerged and stood beside Titan. He knew its shape, knew this tall black stallion as his own beloved Hercules; his kind wide eyes looked down, his shaken mane, his soft mouth smiling. Thomas rose now, turned and flicked his dark cloak aside as he stepped into the stirrup. Benjamin nodded as he passed Thomas his familiar black hat; together they moved their horses forward to halt upon the hilltop.

Thomas' breathing calmed, he heard a faint echo of a stringed instrument in the distance; lost in its melody he fixed his eyes upon the waving figure in the centre of the ship.

'He is gone,' said Benjamin. 'We young men must remain, you and I, we must keep faith here, be strong, work our lands, care for our mother and our younger brothers and sisters.'

Spray from the surging waters clung to the breezes leaving a salty taste upon their lips. The ship leaned hard amidst the rising waves, its boards creaking, the sound riding, merging, enfolding amongst the faint echoes of distant strings.

'We shall,' said Thomas, '…and later, when we hear from him, we shall follow. We shall all follow.'

Give and Take: Lace...
Judith Tomlinson

1680s, Pas de Calais

Abraham held his young wife close but his words were of little comfort. 'Marie, please, please don't weep. We really must leave while we have life and limb. The king has taken away our protection of the Edict*. Jacob says there have been people slaughtered only a day's journey away — the new Bishop is stirring hatred.'

Marie looked fearfully at her husband, so many thoughts tearing her jagged mind apart. She knew he was right — if they were to keep their faith and their lives, they had to go, leaving all that was familiar behind, but where would they find safety? How would they survive?

The following daybreak, they joined others from their congregation. The laden carts creaked and growled their way to the coast. Never had she seen so much water. Marie shivered at the thought they may have escaped murder, only to drown. She buried her face, first into Abraham's cloak and then into her hands as she prayed harder than she thought she had ever prayed, that the Lord would deliver them to safety.

There was a collective sigh of relief when the boat reached shelter in a harbour flanked by haughty white cliffs. They were weary and still anxious, despite the reassurances of some merchants who had made this crossing many times. Marie and Abraham climbed from the boat, bewildered by their surroundings and the unfathomable speech of the people on the bustling harbour side. They stayed close to others seeking refuge, including a few who seemed to have some notion as to what they should do. Soon, carts were hired and loaded with their possessions.

In the early evening, they reached their destination. People who spoke their language — merchants who had travelled back and forth — helped them find homes, close to the huge, handsome church. They were invited to worship in an area set aside for Strangers, mostly Huguenots like themselves. It was a comfort to follow the familiar pattern of worship, though hurt and anxiety were never far away.

While most of their possessions had been left in Valenciennes, Marie soon found the fine Flemish style lace she produced was in demand, while Abraham, a cordwainer*, was invited to join with Jacob Masquelir, the friend who had warned him of the approaching danger back in Pas de Calais.

They worked hard and, while often thinking about those they had left behind, now felt their future lay in England, where they now had many friends, not just from their faith. Their children spoke English, were English. Some married out of the faith. The family spread from Canterbury. Only the family name, Faidherbe, identified their origin and even that changed as the years went by. Living in Whitstable, Horatio, their great, great grandson became a master mariner, with none of his great, great grandmother's trepidation at venturing on to the high seas. His son, James, sailed into the Southern Oceans.

England had given the young couple, Marie and Abraham, safety and their descendants a future filled with opportunity.

The Edict of Nantes was introduced by Henry IV in 1584, helping end the decades of religious wars, by reinstating Protestant rights on encouraging tolerance. It was revoked by Louis XIV in 1685, provoking an exodus of thousands of Huguenots, including many skilled craftspeople.

A cordwainer is a shoemaker.

... and Flax

*1840, Aotearoa**

It was a wonderful garment, made from flax, with such care and love by his wife and daughters. It made him feel powerful and ready to act on behalf of his people.

He led the elders to the meeting place. The pale men, whom they called pakehas, approached. Their spokesman, who, on a previous trading visit, had told them about their special God and his loving son, explained that he came in peace, on behalf of a mighty Queen far away. He said what his masters proposed would benefit the people of both lands. The trader's words were strange and the ideas he described were complicated, with much being lost in translation. His beautiful flaxen cloak failed to help him grasp the enormity of the situation, though he had grave doubts as he put his mark on the document.

James Williamson Fedarb, trading master of the Bay of Islands schooner Mercury completed his voyage around the Bay of Plenty between 22 May and 19 June 1840, collecting assent from Maori chiefs at Opotiki, Te Kaha, Torere and Whakatane.

A man whose antecedents had been given refuge in England one hundred and fifty years previously, played an important part in the completion of the Treaty of Waitangi, assisting in the taking, however honourable his reasons, of land and independence from the Maori people.

* Aotearoa is the Maori name for New Zealand, translated as Land of the Long White Cloud.

A Cat May Look at a King (but it can be unwise)
Roger Brandon

Whenever I visit RAMM I always have to start with a tour of my old favourites from the early days of the museum.

First stop is the Sladen collection of slimy things, that quintessentially Victorian grouping of sea creatures, in jars of formaldehyde or dissected and dried. It houses some of the most disgusting objects in the museum. I have a soft spot for the sea urchins. As children we would find them on the beaches, and called them "Bishop's Mitres". It turns out the hole in the top we blew through is the anus.

Then on to say hello to Gerald, the giraffe, and the elephant. I always thought there were bones inside until I went on a conducted tour and learnt the hunters just brought the skins back. The insides are all wood, wire, and plaster. Obvious, I suppose. I am sorry the iconic Gerald has been relegated to a dark room instead of his old place of honour.

The next "must-see" is the 19th century Inuit waterproof parker, a wonderful garment made from seal gut stitched with human hair. They took around a month to make, but the information board doesn't say how many seals it took. I can't help thinking it took a lot of guts to make one.

Now it is time to wander around before finishing up with my favourite animal. I visit the new exhibitions, but take time to revisit the 'regulars' as there are always new and useless facts to find which I had missed before. The blood of the Horseshoe Crab is bright blue, being full of copper and not iron, as in most animals. Star fish have up to thirty arms and can reproduce missing parts; some voluntarily break up their bodies to produce a complete twin of themselves.

Enough of this. I am sure it could drive you mad eventually, and I am tired. It is time to have a sit and talk to my favourite — the Bengal tiger.

The tiger is also representative of his age, being one of thirty-nine shot in Nepal by George V in 1911 as he and his party sat on elephants and had the tigers beaten towards him. Still, one must give him credit, he donated one to the museum so poor people who couldn't go to India could see one.

I sit, suck a sweet, and look into those baleful glass eyes that aren't quite appropriate for one of the world's most dangerous animals. I can imagine what it was like for him, terrified and confused. I wonder what it was like for the beaters...

The Beater's Story.

Guar Chand was working in the fields with the other men when Durga Charen , accompanied by two assistants, came to the village, twirling his moustache and swinging the ebony cane that had been given to him by an English sahib. The women ran to fetch the old men, who were sitting smoking outside the workshop where Suchet made pots and pans and knives. They shouted to the children to go to the fields and fetch their fathers. Durga Charen didn't say anything, but sat on the chair brought out for him and took the drink offered. He didn't need to say why he was there, everyone knew.

Durga Charen organised shoots for the English sahibs. When it was a big one he would come out to the villages to recruit beaters. He sat and drank and smoked and talked with the old men about the tiger hunts in the days of the Maharaja, whilst he waited for the men to come in from the fields. He also told them how the new Sahibs often sat all night in *manchans* high up in the trees, and put an animal carcass below as bait. He laughed scornfully and gave his moustache an extra twirl. More often than not nothing came and the Sahibs spent a cold and uncomfortable night. They did not dare to come down until daybreak, when the tigers slept; not daring to sleep themselves in case a snake climbed their tree. But not this hunt. This would be a proper hunt, in daylight, on elephants.

Once the men had come in from the fields and were assembled Durga Charen rose to his feet and addressed them with great solemnity. 'Today you are blessed with a great occasion. Today is a day your children's children will talk about. Today I am organising the greatest tiger hunt ever, for no less a noble Englishman than the King himself.' There was an excited babble. It was known that King George was visiting India, but that he should come to this area! There was a clamour of men wanting to be beaters and after some deliberation, and acceptance of a goat, Durga Charen chose twelve. He had other villages to visit, and other gifts to accept.

Guar Chand was one of the twelve, and on the first day of the shoot he and the others assembled at a point by the river. The scouts had been tracking tigers all week and knew where several were sleeping during the day. Senior beaters took groups of men into the jungle and lined them up with their heavy sticks. At the signal they started beating the undergrowth, shouting, and blowing whistles and horns. They moved forward, always keeping the beaters on each side in view.

Away to his right Guar Chand could see Bahadur Khan from his village. He was one of the few who carried a gun, a muzzle-loading "Brown Bess" which had somehow found its way from the army into his hands. He, and others who had guns, fired into the air at intervals, but he was not allowed to put ball into his musket. Men from the army were also there, with new guns that fired special bullets called "blanks".

They walked towards the area where one of the sleeping tigers lay. Now he was awake, they could hear him growling angrily. They were to beat the tiger towards the elephants which were slowly moving through the jungle in a line abreast.

It took a long time before the tiger was driven into the line of elephants, and great trouble was taken to steer it towards the elephant that had the honour of carrying the King. This was the time of most danger. Tigers might attack the elephant or the men in the *howdah*. Sometimes the hunter would find himself literally face to face with his prey. It was also a time of greatest danger for the men on the ground. The circle of beaters was now quite tight. If the hunters did not kill it the wounded tiger would charge through the encircling men. But that was not the only danger.

Englishmen could be quite excitable and sometimes shot at any movement in the undergrowth, and that might include a beater. This was not always a tragedy. If the beater were shot in the arm or leg he must lie on the ground and say he cannot move it. He must wail that his children will starve. The Sahib will then give him very many rupees, and with luck he will only have a stiff arm or a limp. If the beater is killed that will be terrible, but the elder of the village will bargain for hundreds of rupees, and will then make sure his family is looked after.

Up in the *howdah* the royal party were tense and nervous. There were three guns, and two of them knew they must hold fire and let the King take the first shot. With a suddenness that caught them all by surprise the tiger burst into view. He would have disappeared into the jungle again in a bound, but it heard the beaters ahead and hesitated. In that moment the King fired. The tiger staggered, looked up at where the noise had come from, then turned to run, but three more shots followed. It sprang into the air, before falling on the ground with just its paws twitching.

A hunter climbed down from one of the elephants and gingerly approached the animal, which was still giving an occasional twitch. He fired at close range. The tiger lay still. As the beaters shouted 'Bag mahrgaya' (the tiger is dead) the Royal elephant sank to his knees and the King climbed down to survey the beast. They measured it from its nose to the tip of its tail and called out it was almost nine feet long. The beaters were marshalled into a group and the King placed a foot on the tiger, whilst several photographs were taken. Then he thanked everyone and the party left to go to a new area in the hope of killing another tiger before the day was ended. As they left, the skinners started. Once tanned, some of the skins would be presented to the King's hosts, but others would be taken back to England.

It was two weeks later that Durga Charen came back to the village to pay the beaters. He said the King alone had shot thirty-nine tigers. His majesty would take most of the skins home to be rugs in the palaces, or to give to important people. But he had been told that some would be given to museums. There they would be stuffed and mounted for English people to look at. It seems, and here a note of incredulity came into Durga Charen's voice, there were no tigers in England.

The Toran
Sharon Cook

Objects define us, place us — trace us — connect us...

A 'toran' is a doorway hanging that divides an internal space into the sacred and secular. These hangings help to promote fertility and protection with their hanging pendants and dazzling reflective surfaces.

What if? What if this humble Toran could take us right back to the beginning – the very beginning, back to the darkness, to the birth of life itself? If I were to tell you a traveller's tale, would you believe me? Could you understand I have travelled in time just to bring you a taste of the exotic, a trace of the mysterious? There is barbary, there is spirituality, mystery and romance, pain and suffering – and all from far, far away.

This is a tale of soldiers and travellers, of missionaries and merchants of a scientist and of souvenir hunters who have proved themselves to be the most ruthless of all.

First there was the darkness — then there was the Toran.

You must be initiated – you must know of the Toran, sacred to all who pass beneath her.

My grandmother's Toran hung over the doorway of her living and dying room, the doorway into her kitchen. Her kitchen was a place of smells, of love, of comfort and of Rajasthani culture. Here in Rajasthan we believe in many things. For us the Toran blesses those who pass beneath and the Toran offers fertility – of the soul and of the body. It offers protection.

Many Holy Men blessed my grandmother's Toran, far more spiritual women claimed its blessings. The pointed pendant hung above the heads of all but the very tallest; it hung as a reminder to all that we were loved and we were blessed.

My grandmother was a healer, of bodies and of souls. My grandmother could trace her ancestry to the beginning, to the beginning of all souls who ever walked, or crawled, or swam, or slithered or flew through the skies.

First there was the darkness — then there was the Toran.

My grandmother's Toran was bright of earth colours — rich reds, ochres and green pure as the ripe tea leaves growing on the plains, as green as the rice paddies in full leaf. Without the orange of the skies our Toran would not have sparked the tiny mirror buttons of mica, capturing the rays of the sun on even the dullest of days.

It was my great great grandmother who stitched her daughter's Toran, the redness of the thread faded over time, but the vibrancy of the colours and the patterns will remain with me until my dying day, which is not far off. So we must hurry — I must tell you my tale before my grandmother's living and dying room becomes my own.

I remember the stripes of some of the patches and though my eyes have faded into the darkness — I remember every one of the ten tiny patches, stitched together, the deep scarlet of the pointed pendant a permanent fixture in my head.

The colours are taking me away from the darkness, my fading eyesight the victim of cataracts. It's always the darkness, so the end defines the beginning.

In the beginning there was the darkness which, in truth, birthed us all.